An art contest with high stakes

What came next on the TV program was the biggest news of all.

The art teacher spoke directly into the microphone. "On Thursday, three days from now, I will ask a handful of third and fourth graders to share their art posters on this TV station. Next week I'll ask the younger children."

Room 3B turned quiet.

Go on TV?

Suddenly, our room broke out in cheers. We could hear other kids clapping and cheering from rooms down the hall.

"Oh," Mary sighed. "I've always wanted to go on television. This is my big chance!"

Mary took out her package of sixty-four crayons from her art supply box and admired their good condition.

"I'm ready to make the best poster!" she announced.

OTHER BOOKS IN THE HORRIBLE HARRY SERIES

HORRIBLE HARRY
and the Scarlet Scissors

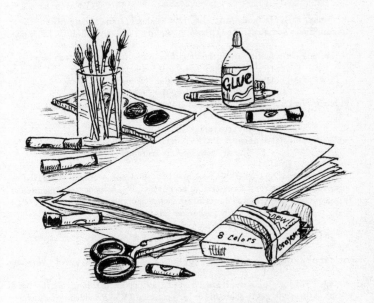

BY **SUZY KLINE**
PICTURES BY **AMY WUMMER**

PUFFIN BOOKS
An Imprint of Penguin Group (USA) Inc.

PUFFIN BOOKS
An imprint of Penguin Young Readers Group
Published by the Penguin Group
Penguin Group (USA) Inc.
375 Hudson Street
New York, New York 10014, U.S.A.

USA / Canada / UK / Ireland / Australia / New Zealand / India / South Africa / China
Penguin Books Ltd, Registered Offices: 80 Strand, London WC2R 0RL, England

For more information about the Penguin Group visit www.penguin.com

First published in the United States of America by Viking,
a division of Penguin Young Readers Group, 2012
Published by Puffin Books, an imprint of Penguin Young Readers Group, 2013

Text copyright © Suzy Kline, 2012
Illustrations copyright © Viking Children's Books, 2012
Illustrations by Amy Wummer

All rights reserved. No part of this book may be reproduced, scanned, or distributed
in any printed or electronic form without permission. Please do not participate in or
encourage piracy of copyrighted materials in violation of the author's rights. Purchase
only authorized editions.

THE LIBRARY OF CONGRESS HAS CATALOGED THE VIKING EDITION AS FOLLOWS:
Kline, Suzy.
Horrible Harry and the scarlet scissors / by Suzy Kline ; illustrated by Amy Wummer.
p. cm.—(Horrible Harry ; 28)
Summary: "The kids in Room 3B are asked to draw posters of things that they love,
and one of them will get to share his or her poster on TV"—Provided by publisher.
ISBN 978-0-670-01306-7 (hardback)
[1. Contests—Fiction. 2. Drawing—Fiction. 3. Schools—Fiction. 4. Behavior—Fiction.]
I. Wummer, Amy, ill. II. Title.
PZ7.K6797Hnsc 2012 [E]—dc23 2011035952

Puffin Books ISBN 978-0-14-242671-5

Printed in the United States of America

1 3 5 7 9 10 8 6 4 2

The publisher does not have any control over and does not assume any responsibility
for author or third-party websites or their content.

To my beautiful granddaughter,
Kenna Rose Hurtuk,
who had lots of fun making an art poster
at her school. Keep being a wonderful writer!
I love you,
Gamma

Special appreciation to . . .

Noah Wallace School in Farmington, Connecticut, for inspiring this story. I loved the unicorn posters in the hallways!

And heartfelt appreciation to Randy Sparks and Barry McGuire, of the New Christy Minstrels, for allowing me to use the lyrics from their wonderful song "Green, Green."

And to many Southwest School students in Torrington, Connecticut, for responding to the quotation *Beauty is in the eye of the beholder*.

And appreciation for two great thinkers: Plato, who inspired the famous quotation in this book, and Leo Tolstoy, who wrote the wonderful essay "What Is Art?"

I also want to thank my dear husband, Rufus, for his valuable suggestions.

And very special thanks to my perceptive editor, Leila Sales, for the conversations we had about this book. Her thoughtful criticism and questions greatly helped me write this story.

Contents

Harry the Horrible Artist

My name is Doug. I write stories about my friend Harry and me in Room 3B. I never thought I'd be writing about an art show.

Harry and art?

Are you kidding?

Harry and I are not good artists. Actually, Harry is a horrible artist. And although he loves horrible things, he can't draw them. His pictures of snakes and worms look like sticks. So if you were to tell me Harry's work was going to be in an art show, I would say . . .

That is *not* going to happen!

But it did.

You have to read this story to find out *how*.

There are plenty of surprises along the way. And the ending? Well, it was on TV!

It all started one Monday morning, a few days before Saint Patrick's Day. Kids in Room 3B were taking off their coats, hats, and gloves. Harry was looking out the window at the school playground and the vacant lot just beyond the school fence. "Oh, man," he groaned. "The snow is still everywhere. I can't believe it's the second week of March! Where's the grass, anyway?"

Mary was at her desk, showing Song Lee and Ida her little doll. It had lots of hair. Mary reached for her art supply box. "I'm going to trim my doll's bangs with these," she said, holding up a pair of scissors with red handles. "My brand-new scarlet scissors!"

"Ohhh . . . scarlet," Ida replied. "I love that bright red color."

"Me too," Song Lee said. "It reminds me of a candy apple." They watched

Mary carefully cut her doll's yellow hair.

Just as the last morning bell rang, our teacher, Miss Mackle, hurried into the classroom. "Boys and girls, get to your seats, please!" she called out. "At nine o'clock, South School is going on TV!"

"TV? Yahoo!" Sid blurted out.

Song Lee and Ida quickly returned to their seats.

South School on TV? That's a first! I thought.

Harry plopped in his chair. He sat between Mary and me. "Have you guys seen any grass that's *not* covered with snow?" he moaned.

I shook my head.

Mary didn't answer Harry's question until she had put her doll in her backpack and brushed the yellow doll hairs off her desk. "Harry," she finally replied. "How can you talk about the grass right now? We're going on TV!" Then she took out her hand mirror and checked her teeth.

Harry just shrugged.

Miss Mackle reached for the remote control and clicked the ON button. "Keep your eyes on the screen, boys and girls," she ordered. "Oh, I'm so excited!"

We were all excited, too—except for Harry.

South School Goes on TV

All of us watched a picture come on the TV screen. It was our school library. The camera zoomed in on two fifth graders, a girl and a boy, sitting at a table. There was a globe next to them.

"Welcome to South School's first TV broadcast," the girl said. "My name is Bria, and this is Kemba." The boy waved. "We're *not* just going to read the lunch menu, or tell you the weather, or whose birthday it is. We are going to talk about what's new at South School."

Kemba continued, "And we begin with exciting news! South School has a new art teacher. Please welcome Mrs. Matalata!"

Everyone in Room 3B clapped. We never had an art teacher before! We watched a woman wearing a long, flowing, colored scarf join the fifth graders at the table.

"You have an interesting name," Bria said. "What nationality is Matalata?"

"Indonesian," the art teacher replied.

Bria reached for the

nearby globe and pointed to a group of islands. The camera panned in on the South Pacific area. "Indonesia is near the Philippines, Malaysia, and Australia," she said.

"How cool to be from the South Pacific!" Sid blurted out.

"Shhhh!" Mary scolded. "I don't want to miss a word."

"What advice do you have for kids at South School who want to be good artists?" Kemba asked.

Mrs. Matalata looked at the camera. "Draw what you love."

"All right!" Kemba replied.

Bria smiled. "Are you planning anything special for your first week here at South School?"

"Yes. An art show!" Mrs. Matalata

said. "We're going to make posters and display them throughout the school."

When lots of kids cheered in our room, Harry and I looked at each other.

"Well, that leaves us out," I groaned. "They only pick the best art for art shows."

"That's the way it always is," Harry said, slouching down in his chair.

"What fun!" Bria replied. "Is there a theme, like Saint Patrick's Day? It's coming up this Friday."

Mrs. Matalata shook her head. "No specific theme. I just want students to draw a poster showing something they care about."

"Will there be ribbons and prizes for the best posters?" Kemba asked.

"No. This is not a contest," Mrs. Matalata replied. "Every student will have his or her poster displayed somewhere at South School."

"*Every* student?" Harry and I repeated. Harry sat up.

"Yes!" Sid said, throwing his arms in the air.

"I like our new art teacher!" Ida exclaimed.

Mary rolled her eyes. "Okay, Harry," she said in a low voice, "I hope for your sake your poster is displayed inside a dark closet."

Harry smiled for the first time that morning. "Actually, Mare, I like your idea. That would be a neat place for a poster," he said. "Especially if I draw night crawlers. They love the dark."

Mary cringed. "I was just kidding,

Harry! The inside of a closet is a *horrible* place to hang art!"

I had to laugh.

What came next on the TV program was the biggest news of all.

The art teacher spoke directly into the microphone. "On Thursday, three days from now, I will ask a handful of third and fourth graders to share their art posters on this TV station. Next week, I'll ask the younger children."

Room 3B turned quiet.

Go on TV?

Suddenly, our room broke out in cheers. We could hear other kids clapping and cheering from rooms down the hall.

"Oh," Mary sighed. "I've always wanted to go on television. This is my big chance!"

"Mine, too!" Dexter exclaimed. "I want to be like Elvis. He went on TV and made movies!"

Mary took out her package of sixty-four crayons from her art supply box and admired their good condition. They all had points. Then she pulled out her favorite crayon, burnt sienna, and kissed it. No one ever got to borrow that one. Mary always said it was the perfect blend of red and brown.

"I'm ready to make the best poster!" she announced.

Different Eyeballs

Mrs. Matalata came to Room 3B immediately after the morning broadcast. When she entered our room, it was like she was a rock star. Everyone oohed and ahhed. Her scarf billowed behind her. She wheeled in a cart with a stack of white art paper and brand-new boxes of eight crayons.

Miss Mackle welcomed her with a hug, then left the room.

"Hello, boys and girls!" Mrs. Matala-ta said. "Are you ready to do some art?"

"Yes!" we replied.

Mrs. Matalata wrote something on the board.

Beauty is in the eye of the beholder.

"What do you think this quote means?" she asked.

Ida raised her hand. "I think it means pretty jewelry."

"I don't know what *beholder* means," ZuZu said.

"I do," Sid replied. "A beholder is like the cup holder in your car. Except it's a holder for a bee. A bee holder. Right?"

"No," Mary scoffed. "A beholder is someone who sees something."

"I know what that saying means," Harry blurted out.

We all stared at Harry. What would he know about art? Everybody knew Harry was a horrible artist.

Harry continued, "My grandma says, 'Beauty is in the eye of the beholder' all the time. It means we have different eyeballs."

The art teacher smiled.

I still didn't understand the quote.

Song Lee raised her hand. "I think Harry means that we see things differently."

Mary nodded. "Harry and I definitely see things differently. He thinks hanging a poster in a dark closet is neat! I think it's horrible."

Lots of us laughed, including the art teacher.

"Anyone else?" Mrs. Matalata asked.

ZuZu raised his hand. "I agree with

Harry. We do have different eyeballs. I think Jou Jou, my guinea pig, is beautiful. My sister thinks he's smelly and ugly."

Mrs. Matalata clapped her hands. "Those were perfect examples of how beauty is in the eye of the beholder."

Mary and Zuzu beamed.

"All right!" Dexter exclaimed. "Let's get rockin' and rollin' with art!"

The teacher chuckled. "Okay, now I want you to draw something that *you* think is beautiful."

The room suddenly turned quiet. No one made a mark on their paper.

"I know what I can do!" Harry blurted out.

Mary just made a long face.

Favorite Things

Mary put her hands on her head. "Well, I don't know what to draw on my poster."

"Me, either," lots of us said.

Mrs. Matalata passed out questionnaires. "Filling these out will help you discover what you think is beautiful. Maybe one answer will pop out and inspire you to make a poster."

I looked at the questionnaire. There were fifteen blanks to fill.

My Favorite Things

Please list your favorites for each category:

1. Color _blue_
2. Holiday _rice_
3. Food _rice_
4. Place to visit _new york_
   _____
5. Sport or team _meiem_
   _____
6. Book _feleng naae_
7. Music _____
8. Hobby or activity _faing_
9. Mammal _____
10. Bird _✓_
11. Fish _✓_
12. Amphibian _____
13. Reptile _____
14. Plant _✓_
15. Gemstone _____

"I love listing my favorite things!" Ida said.

"Me too," Song Lee agreed.

While everyone was working, I noticed Harry taking out his old crayon box. It was empty except for one fat green crayon. He shook the crayon out of the box and peeled back the paper. Then he looked at me. "Do you have a pair of scissors, Dougo?" he asked.

"No," I answered, "but Mary does. Ask her."

Harry turned around. He looked at Mary's art supply box on her desk. "Can I borrow those red scissors, Mare?"

"They're *scarlet* scissors," she corrected.

"Scarlet who?" Harry asked. He thought she meant they belonged to another girl.

"Scarlet is a bright red color," Mary insisted. "And haven't you ever heard of the word *please*?"

Harry flashed a toothy smile. "Puhleeeese, Mare?"

She reached over and pulled them out. "You can borrow these, but you have to give them right back. I might need them."

"Thank you," Harry replied. Then he took the scarlet scissors and used one of the tips to gouge holes in the end of his crayon. When he noticed I was watching him, Harry whispered, "I have to get my creative juices going."

"Wouldn't you rather use a pencil?" I asked. "I have extra."

"No thanks, Dougo," Harry replied. He held up his crayon. "This'll do."

Mary looked up from her questionnaire. "Harry, that crayon is creepy. It looks like a ghost's face!"

"Neato, huh?" Harry said.

Mary shivered. "I want my scarlet scissors back."

When Harry handed them to her, Mary examined the ends of the blades. There were green crayon markings on one tip. "Harry Spooger! I'm never loaning you anything again!"

Harry just grinned.

Five minutes later, the art teacher asked, "Did everyone finish the questionnaire?"

"Yes!" we all answered.

"Good!" Mrs. Matalata said. "Please

switch papers with the person sitting next to you. Circle the answer that you like best on that person's list."

Harry and I got to switch lists. We were psyched. Ida and Song Lee were, too. Mary wasn't, though. "Why do I have to sit between two annoying boys!" She groaned.

Poor Sid. He didn't do anything. It was just bad timing—right after Harry got Mary's scarlet scissors dirty.

Sid took a quick look at Mary's list and circled one right away. "I like your hobby!" he exclaimed. "You style hair?"

"My *dolls'* hair," Mary said.

"Do you do people's hair?" he asked.

Mary thought about it. Slowly, she began to smile. "I could."

"Would you do my hair after lunch?" he asked. "We have indoor recess again."

"Sure!" Mary replied, pulling a small notebook out of her desk. "Sidney LaFleur, you are my first booking. I'm putting you down for a twelve thirty appointment. Thank you for launching my new hairstyling business!"

Sid stood up and took a bow.

As soon as Mary looked my way, I quickly turned around. I didn't want my hair done.

I picked up Harry's questionnaire.

When I read his answers, my eyeballs almost popped out!

Hair by Mare

Not only was every answer on Harry's questionnaire written with that creepy green crayon, all his favorite things were green, too!

My Favorite Things

Please list your favorites for each category:

1. Color___GREEN_____

2. Holiday___Saint Patrick's Day_____

3. Food____broccoli_____

4. Place to visit____the Emerald City in____

____The Wizard of Oz_____

5. Sport or team____New York Jets, Boston____

____Celtics_____

6. Book____Lyle, Lyle, Crocodile_____

7. Music____the song "Green, Green"____

8. Hobby or activity____making green slime____

9. Mammal____green sloth_____

10. Bird____parrot_____

11. Fish____green spotted puffer fish_____

12. Amphibian____green poison dart frog____

13. Reptile____green python_____

14. Plant____grass_____

15. Gemstone____green bloodstone_____

There was no way I was going to circle broccoli or green python.

"What song is 'Green, Green'?" I asked.

"You don't know that one?" Harry replied. "My grandma plays it all the time. It's from a New Christy Minstrels album. I love the tune." Harry started singing it:

> *"Green, green, it's green they say*
> *On the far side of the hill.*
> *Green, green, I'm going away*
> *To where the grass is greener still."*

"Well," I said. "I can see why you love that song. It's all about the green grass."

Harry grinned.

I circled Saint Patrick's Day. "Are you wearing something green on Friday?"

"Are you kidding?" Harry answered.

"I am definitely wearing green."

After we exchanged papers again, the art teacher said, "Now I want you to choose *one* favorite thing from your own list and make a poster about it. Maybe your neighbor helped you make this decision. Maybe not. The important thing is that you are excited about it."

"What if you have trouble drawing your favorite thing?" ZuZu asked.

"Yeah," Dexter agreed. "I can't draw Elvis very well."

"You can use resources, like a picture from a book, or if you're drawing a shoe, look at your own," the art teacher suggested. "Study the lines."

"That could help," ZuZu said. He reached for our G encyclopedia.

Dexter put two thumbs up. "You just

gave me a cool idea!" And he took off one shoe and set it on his desk.

Everyone got busy drawing posters. Mary took out her hand mirror and studied her face. She drew a picture of her head, then added a fancy hairdo and three words. The art teacher chuckled when she read them.

"I like your message," she said. "'Hair by Mare.' That's clever."

Mary beamed. "I'm opening up my own beauty salon right here at school."

"I'm her first customer," Sid bragged.

"Client," Mary corrected. "That's what they say in real salons."

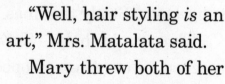

"Well, hair styling *is* an art," Mrs. Matalata said.

Mary threw both of her arms in the air. "Yes!"

The art teacher moved on to Song Lee's desk. "What kind of tree are you drawing?" she asked.

"It's a cherry tree," Song Lee answered softly. "There are lots of those in Korea. That's where my family is from."

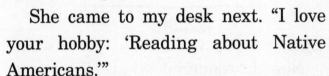

Song Lee Park

"How wonderful," Mrs. Matalata replied.

She came to my desk next. "I love your hobby: 'Reading about Native Americans.'"

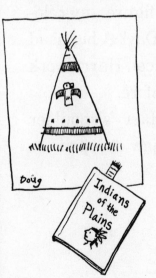

"Thanks," I said. I was drawing birds on my Plains Indians' tepee. I found a good picture of one in my library book.

Sidney was drawing his grand-father's canary perched on his finger. He did a good job on the finger. Sid kept staring at his own as he drew it.

Now I wondered what Harry was drawing. A green stick figure guy celebrating Saint Patrick's Day? A big head of broccoli? I had never seen Harry work so hard on a drawing before.

When I looked over Harry's shoulder and saw his poster, my jaw dropped.

Harry's Shocking Poster

Harry had not touched the new box of crayons that the art teacher gave each of us. He was still using his fat green crayon with the ghostlike face. He kept drawing blades of grass all over his poster. Some were bent, some were leaning on the ground, some were standing tall. It looked like an unmowed lawn you could hide in. At the top was one word: MISSING.

"Wow!" I said. "That's . . . different, Harry." I tried to think of another word besides *shocking*.

"Thanks, Dougo. But I feel like it still needs something. I just don't know what."

"You don't have much room to add anything," I replied. "Your poster is wall to wall grass!"

"*That's* my problem," Harry said.

As soon as everyone finished their poster, Mrs. Matalata asked each of us to talk about our work.

Dexter went first. He had drawn a pair of blue shoes. "Elvis was the King of rock 'n' roll. His version of 'Blue Suede Shoes' was popular in 1956. I have every song he ever sang, but this one is my favorite. I can't draw people well, but I can draw shoes if I'm looking at them."

Mrs. Matalata touched Dexter's poster. "You colored these so dark they feel like blue suede!"

Ida went next. Her poster showed a ballet dancer. It looked just like Ida. "I have been taking lessons since I was four," she said. "I love dancing!"

The art teacher looked closely at her drawing. "I like the detail you put on the girl's tutu, and the musical notes you drew on the side."

When Mrs. Matalata called on Harry, you could hear a pin drop. Everyone wondered what Harry could possibly draw. He held up his grass poster with the one word, MISSING.

Everyone gasped.

"He just used one color," Mary observed. "And one word."

"I wonder how many blades of grass he drew!" Ida said.

"I'd estimate about a thousand," ZuZu replied.

Song Lee clapped her hands silently. She smiled from ear to ear. "It's original!" she exclaimed.

"Winter is too long this year," Harry said. "I miss the grass."

The art teacher put her hand over her heart. "I can feel it!" she said. "That's what art can do—share a feeling."

After everyone talked about their poster, Mrs. Matalata headed for the door.

"Aren't you telling us who gets to go on TV to share their poster?" Mary asked.

"That will be announced on Thursday," the art teacher said. Then she slid a roll of masking tape over her wrist like a bracelet. "Now, let's begin our poster parade. Please line up. We're going to find a place for *everyone's* poster somewhere in the school!"

We jumped out of our seats, grabbed our posters, and hurried to the door.

The Poster Parade

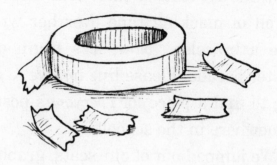

We all followed Mrs. Matalata down the hall. Miss Mackle joined us for the parade. She walked at the end of the line and reminded people to stay together. One by one kids stopped to put up posters. I taped my tepee poster on the library door.

Song Lee taped her cherry tree poster next to the large window in the hallway.

"I don't know where to put my 'Hair by Mare' poster," Mary complained.

"I know where I'm putting my poster," Sid piped up. "The principal's office. Cutey Pie has been there before."

We watched Sid tape his canary poster to Mr. Cardini's door. "See you later, el tweeto," Sid said.

Mary continued to moan. "I have to find the perfect spot to hang my 'Hair by Mare' poster," she repeated.

"I know where you can hang it," Harry said.

"Where?" Mary eagerly asked.

"The bathroom."

"That's gross, Harry!"

"Well, it looks like a hair salon in there," Harry replied. "You need a sink and a mirror."

Mary stopped walking. "People who look in the mirror *are* thinking about their hair," she mumbled.

As soon as the class got downstairs, Mary ducked into the girls' bathroom. The door was propped open, so I could see the row of sinks. She taped her poster right next to the mirror. Then

she skipped out of the bathroom. "I'm launching my hair salon business!" she exclaimed. "Now, after I go on TV and tell everyone about it, I'll really get lots of clients!"

ZuZu hung his poster of Jou Jou, his guinea pig, on the boiler room door. "Jou Jou likes small warm places," ZuZu said.

"I like the words you put on your poster, ZuZu," Miss Mackle said. "'Be Kind to Your Pets.'"

Dexter hung his poster over the lost-and-found table. "Elvis's blue suede shoes go well with all this stuff," he said.

When Ida hung her ballet poster in the gym, Mr. Deltoid, our phys ed teacher, stood up on his toes and twirled around. "Bravo!" he called out.

Miss Mackle clapped as he danced.

After we got back to our classroom, the art teacher started to say good-bye.

She thought all the posters were displayed.

"But Harry didn't put up his poster!" I objected.

"Oh, goodness," Mrs. Matalata said.

"Don't worry about it," Harry replied. "I know exactly where I want to hang it."

We all watched Harry walk over to the classroom closet, open it up, and tape his poster to the inside of the door. Then he closed it. "Done!" he said.

"Are you sure you want to put it there?" Miss Mackle asked. "No one will be able to see it."

"Positive," Harry replied. Then he flashed a toothy smile.

Mary shook her head. "I can't believe Harry really did that," she mumbled. "I was kidding!"

Both teachers exchanged a look, and then chuckled.

"Thanks, boys and girls, for being such hardworking artists," Mrs. Matalata called out.

"Thank you," we all replied.

Mary crossed both her fingers. "Ohh, I hope I get picked to go on TV. I have to!"

After everyone had lunch, it was time for indoor recess. Mary styled Sid's hair. She used a comb and a paper cup of water from our sink. When she was done, she gave Sid her hand mirror.

"I love it!" Sid said. "I look like Dexter." Sid's hairdo was combed back and slick like Elvis.

"Cool 'do, Mare," Harry said as he passed by.

"Way cool," Dexter agreed.

Mary beamed. "Do you want to be next, Dexter?"

"Nooooo!" he replied. "My hair is like Elvis's blue suede shoes. He sings, 'Don't step on my blue suede shoes.' I sing, 'Don't mess with my hair, baby!'"

"I get it," Mary groaned. "I don't need your business. I have other clients lined up."

Mary put Ida's hair in a ponytail with a scarf around it. Then Mary took her pig and dog magneto pals off her book bag and attached them to each of Song Lee's pigtails.

Mary stepped back and admired her hair creations. "Just a few days more, girls, and it's TV time!"

Oh boy, I thought. *I hope Mary does go on TV, because if she doesn't, there's going to be a* huge *Mary tantrum in Room 3B!*

The Big TV Show

Two days later, it was Thursday, the day before Saint Patrick's Day. The day we would find out who would get to go on South School's TV station to talk about their poster. I could tell everyone was excited. When Harry and I were getting a drink in Room 3B, the girls rushed in, squealing.

"I love it!" Ida exclaimed.

"You look beautiful!" Song Lee said

to Mary. All three girls were jumping up and down.

Mary's hair was really curly.

"Mom gave me a new perm last night. Just in time." Mary lowered her voice. "Just in case I might go on TV!" Then she squealed again.

I kept my fingers crossed for Mary, and for myself. It would be really neat to go on TV and talk about the Plains Indians. I could show the whole school how they live in tepees. But I also wanted Mary to win. There would be no peace in Room 3B if she didn't.

Dexter strutted into class wearing a shirt with Elvis on it. He had added extra gel to his hair. I could tell he was hoping to go on TV, too.

As we sat there waiting for the

morning show to come on, Harry whispered, "See you later, Doug. I have to go bad."

Harry dashed out the door like it was a bathroom emergency.

Miss Mackle turned on the TV. "There's Bria!" Mary called out as the camera panned the library.

Bria and Kemba were sitting at the table. "Welcome, South School. We bring you special news!" Kemba exclaimed.

"It's time for the first televised South School Art Show," Bria continued. "Mrs. Matalata?"

The camera moved to the art teacher. "All of the third and fourth graders did a terrific job with their posters. Today, I would like to feature five posters that were real attention grabbers.

They make you stop and think. These posters also have lots of feeling."

We recognized only one.

Mary slouched in her chair as she blew up her curly bangs. It wasn't hers.

"It's Harry's!" we all shouted. There was his grass poster!

The class looked back at Harry's desk. He wasn't there.

"Where's Harry?" Song Lee blurted out. I could tell she was worried. She never talks without being called on.

"Don't worry, boys and girls," Miss Mackle said. "Harry's in the library."

Suddenly Harry appeared on TV! When the camera panned in on his face, Harry

flashed a toothy smile. Then the camera zoomed in on the blades of grass on Harry's poster and the one word at the top, MISSING.

Harry brought the microphone to his mouth. "When Mrs. Matalata said we could draw what we love, I knew right away what it was. The grass! I really miss it. I also miss looking for earwigs and night crawlers. Those are beautiful things to me," he said.

After the other four kids shared their posters, Harry returned to Room 3B. Everyone clapped. Except Mary. She was frozen in her chair and gritting her teeth. She looked like a time bomb ready to go off!

Mary and the Scarlet Scissors

"Way to go, Harry!" I said, greeting him at the door. Harry had his poster under his arm. Song Lee and Ida dashed over to him and gave him a hug.

"How was it?" Miss Mackle asked.

Harry shrugged.

"You had about three hundred and forty kids watching you, Harry!" ZuZu said. "That's how many there are at South School."

Song Lee and Ida were still clapping their hands for Harry.

"Thanks, guys," Harry said. "But it was no biggie. It's just like being in the library, only I didn't check out a book."

Mary folded her arms. She hadn't moved from her desk. "It's no fair," she mumbled. "Harry doesn't even appreciate going on TV. It should have been me!"

Harry set his poster down on his desk. "Boy, I need a drink after all that talking," he said, and walked over to the water faucet by the classroom sink.

Miss Mackle began writing math problems on the board. "Please copy these in your math journal. It's time to practice multiplication."

Mary reached for her scarlet scissors.

She turned and faced Harry's empty desk.

What is she up to? I wondered.

I looked at Mary, and then at her scarlet scissors. The blades were spread apart. There was still a little green crayon line on one of the tips. Mary took Harry's poster, held it up, and then stabbed it!

My eyes bulged. There were two slashes right in the middle of Harry's art paper!

I looked around.

Did anyone else see?

Not the teacher. She had her back to the class. She was still writing math problems.

Everyone else was copying them down except for one person. Song Lee.

When our eyes met, I could tell we both had the same thought.

How could Mary do that?

Song Lee covered her eyes.

I couldn't believe it.

Mary couldn't believe it, either. She immediately dropped her scarlet scissors. The poster slipped out of her hands onto the floor. Mary collapsed into her chair. When I looked up, Harry was on his way back from the drinking fountain. *Oh boy*, I thought.

Harry sat down and wiped water off his mouth. Then he bent over and picked up his poster from the floor.

"There's still something missing in my picture, Doug," he said, and he held it up.

He looked long and hard at his poster.

The two holes were right in the middle.

"Hey," Harry said. "Who did this?"

The Hole Truth

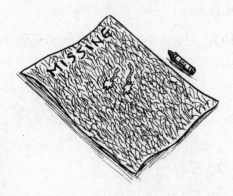

I looked over at Mary. She had her head buried on her desk. Very slowly, she sat up and turned toward Harry. "I did it," she whispered. There were tears in her eyes. "I'm so sorry, Harry. As soon as I did it, I knew it was wrong. I was just so jealous about you going on TV. Can I tape the holes up for you? I have transparent tape."

Harry shook his head.

He was still looking straight ahead at his poster. He didn't say a word. He just kept looking at those holes.

Suddenly Harry blurted out, "I've got it!"

Sidney looked up from his math. "Hey," he said, "who ruined Harry's poster?"

Miss Mackle turned around. "Is there a problem?"

Everyone looked up from their math journals. The teacher walked over to Harry's desk. "What happened to your poster?" she asked.

Mary was shaking. She was terrified. She started to say something, but Harry interrupted her.

"I forgot the night crawlers," Harry said. "So I made two holes in the grass.

Now all I need is a brown crayon."

Mary looked the other way. She probably didn't want the teacher to see her tears.

Miss Mackle sighed. "It's your poster, Harry. Okay, boys and girls, continue working on your math." And she went back to the board. "That includes you, Harry," she added.

"I knew my poster was missing something," Harry whispered.

Mary reached for a crayon in her art supply box. I couldn't believe it! It was burnt sienna, her favorite. She handed it to Harry.

"It really is a good worm color," she said softly.

Harry grinned. "Thanks, Mare!"

Harry drew two worms coming out of the holes on his poster. "I love it!" he exclaimed. "Now this is a picture that is *really* about something beautiful!" And he walked to the closet and taped it back to the inside of the door.

"Oh Harry," Mary said when he returned. "Do you know how sorry I am?"

Harry reached down and picked up the scarlet scissors from the floor. He handed them to her. "Yes," he said. "I know."

"I would be so angry if someone did that to my paper," Mary said. "You should never ever touch someone's artwork. I can't stand the ugly feeling I have inside me."

Harry lowered his voice. "Mare," he said, "I love my poster now with night crawler holes. I forgot to put them in. So it worked out great."

Mary leaned over and whispered,

"Please let me do something to make it up. It would make me feel better."

Harry thought about it, then he whispered something in Mary's ear.

Mary smiled. "Sure. I can do that tomorrow before school. I'll have my mom drop me off at your house."

Tomorrow at Harry's house?

"What's going on, Harry?" I asked.

He just grinned. "It's a Saint Patrick's Day surprise, Dougo."

A Beautiful Ending

The next morning was Saint Patrick's Day. Song Lee tied green ribbons and shamrocks in her hair. Ida wore a green necklace. Sid had a plastic green Derby hat. I wore green socks.

I couldn't wait for Harry and Mary to arrive. What was their surprise? I stood at the bottom of the ramp, watching the parents drop kids off for school.

Song Lee, Ida, and Sidney were

nearby, waiting in the tetherball line while ZuZu and Dexter took their turn.

Finally Grandma Spooger's red truck pulled up in front of the school.

Harry and Mary got out of the cab.

I had to look twice.

Harry's hair was spiked green!

"Have fun today!" Harry's grandma called out. Harry and Mary waved back at her, then ran down the ramp.

"Hi, everyone!" Harry shouted. Lots of kids stared at him.

"HARRY HAS GREEN HAIR!" Sid screamed.

Dexter and ZuZu stopped playing tetherball.

We all gathered around Harry. His entire outfit was green. He even smelled green.

"How do you like my 'do?" Harry asked everyone.

"It's Hair by Mare," Mary bragged. "Harry asked me for a green hairdo for Saint Patrick's Day."

"I love it!" Ida cheered.

"It's wild and fun!" Song Lee exclaimed.

I stared at Harry. "You're green from head to toe!" I said.

"I used green markers on my tennis shoes. Grandma got me the washable kind."

"Will that green wash out of your hair?" ZuZu asked.

Harry shrugged.

"Of course," Mary answered. "This is my Saint Pat's holiday special. I mixed green Kool-Aid with hair gel."

So *that's* why he smelled green. It was the lime smell from the Kool-Aid!

"Call me Green Man!" Harry proclaimed.

ZuZu and Dexter slapped Harry five.

"You're a real Boston Celtics fan," ZuZu said, admiring his extra-large green jacket.

"Of course I'm a fan," Harry replied. "And so is my Grampa Spooger. This is his jacket. He let me borrow it for Saint Patrick's Day."

"Those camouflage pants remind me of my uncle," Sid said. "He's an army sergeant."

Harry lifted his jacket so we could see that his T-shirt underneath had green spots.

"That's mold. The shirt got left in the

damp basement, but I knew I'd have a use for it sometime. I was right. You're looking at natural green!"

"Ewyee!" we squealed.

As soon as the school bell rang, we got our book bags and walked into the building. Everyone in the halls stared at Harry. He was a green celebrity!

When the principal saw us in the hallway, he hollered, "Bravissimo, Harry!"

Miss Mackle greeted Harry at the classroom door. She had big green earrings on.

"I'm Green Man," Harry said.

The teacher smiled. "You sure are!" she replied.

As we headed over to the coat rack to hang up our coats, Mary had a word with Harry.

"Thanks for forgiving me, Harry," she whispered. "But I also want to thank you for something else. As it turns out, I didn't need to go on TV to launch my hair business. Two of my neighbors who go to South School saw my poster in the girls' bathroom. They asked me to come over to their house and do their hair! And you . . . well, you are a walking advertisement for me, Harry! I just got five new bookings in the hallway. I even had to tell a dozen kids I just do green hair on Saint Patrick's Day, and then only if their parents say yes."

"All right, Mare," Harry said. "I love my Saint Patrick's Day hairdo." Then he looked at me. "It's a beauty, don't you think, Doug?"

Not to me, I thought. Harry's head looked like a green stegosaurus with all

67

those hairy spikes. But I wasn't going to tell him that. I just slapped Harry five.

Mary beamed. "I think it's beautiful," she said. "It's my favorite hair creation so far!"

Did Mary and Harry's eyeballs just agree on something?

Yes! Harry's spiked green hair!

Whoa . . . that will probably not happen again for a long time. Maybe not until next Saint Patrick's Day.

And then, just like every morning, Harry walked over to the window and checked the scene outside. Suddenly, he was jumping up and down. "I SEE THE GRASS!" he yelled.

Song Lee dashed over to the window. "I SEE IT, TOO!" she squealed.

Now *that*, to my eyes, was beautiful!

2 1982 02843 6537